To the Sherwood Foundation and my Nebraska friends: Nancy Larimer,
Beverly Kay Doeschot, Laura Pietsch, Kathleen Day, Stephany Albritton,
Stacy Sanders, Sherry Bergen, and Kim McCain

ISBN 978-0-545-84900-5

Copyright © 2014 by David Biedrzycki.
All rights reserved. Published by
Scholastic Inc., 557 Broadway, New York, NY 10012,
by arrangement with Charlesbridge Publishing, Inc.
SCHOLASTIC and associated logos are
trademarks and/or registered trademarks
of Scholastic Inc.

12 11 10 9 8 7 6 5 4 3 2 1     15 16 17 18 19 20/0

Printed in the U.S.A.              40

First Scholastic printing, February 2015

Illustrations done in Adobe Photoshop
Display type set in The Sans by Luc as de Groot
Text type set in Stripwriter by Typotheticals
Designed by Diane M. Earley

**BREAKING NEWS**

# BEAR ALERT

*Reported by* **David Biedrzycki**

BEAR ALERT SKYCAM 3 NEWS HELICOPTER SHOWS TWO

BEARS ON TOP OF TRUCK HEADED DOWNTOWN.

**TRAFFIC CAMERA CAPTURES SHOWDOWN.** *BEAR ALERT*

Teddy's Diner security video

<EXIT>

NO BARE FEET PLEASE WAIT TO BE SEATED

*BEAR ALERT* BEARS SEEN ENTERING TEDDY'S DINER.

ENTER

CAUTION CAUTION

CAUTION CAUTION

WET CEMENT

Pooh St.

Main S

DETOUR
BEAR RIGHT

*BEAR ALERT* SKYCAM 3 NEWS HELICOPTER SPOTS BEARS

ROUNDING THE CORNER OF POOH AND MAIN.

THESE BEARS ARE WILD AND COULD BE EXTREMELY DANGEROUS.

**BEAR ALERT** EXPERTS SAY BEARS ARE NATURALLY SHY AND

**LOUD SOUNDS WILL SCARE THEM AWAY.** *BEAR ALERT*

**BEAR ALERT** RESIDENTS ARE ASKED TO KEEP THEIR

**BEAR ALERT** ANIMAL CONTROL OFFICERS HAVE ARRIVED

Paddington's security video

**BEAR ALERT** **BEARS LAST SEEN IN MISSES AND PETITES**

**SECTION OF PADDINGTON'S DEPARTMENT STORE.**

**BREAKING NEWS** REPORTED BURGLARY AT PADDINGTON'S.

**SKYCAM 3 SPOTS SUSPECTS FLEEING ON FOOT.**

BREAKING NEWS BEARS NAB BURGLARS. SKYCAM 3

SHOWS POLICE CLOSING IN TO MAKE ARREST.

WE NOW RETURN YOU TO YOUR REGULARLY SCHEDULED STORY.